M AND N

Ben Clitch

contents

1. "Marcus, call Her over,"

"**M**ichael, I'm getting sick and tired of you."

"Just leave him be, Marcus, he said he didn't want to come."

"It's his birthday! He doesn't have a choice but to celebrate."

I let out a long, and hard sigh, lazily tilting my head to look out of the car window. It was true, the last place I wanted to be, was here. In the car, with four of my closest friends as they drove me to hell knows where. Turning 26 wasn't something I wanted to celebrate, I felt old.

"Slap a smile on your face so maybe you'll actually get some tonight, ey?"

Marcus and his stupid British accent. I wanted to push the smile into the back of his face, but I couldn't do that so instead I just kept staring outside of the window.

We arrive at the club after ten minutes, and I lean back harshly into the chair, bringing them all to face me.

"Why the fuck am I here?" I grunt.

"I don't dance, I don't like loud music, I don't drink, so why am I here?"

"Relax, Michael. You're here because tonight is so much more than just club dancing,"

"He's right," Hane joins in with a nod, "tonight those we're gonna be enjoying some strip tease."

I shake my head, beyond annoyed.

There were things that were your things, things you enjoy doing, things you can tolerate, and then there were other things that utterly irritated your spirit. And clubbing was one of those things for me. I didn't see the sense, nor the point in any of it, and frankly, I just wanted to go home.

"You're welcome to stay in the hot vehicle while we get drunk, but you won't do that, right mike?"

"If you call me Mike again, I'll make you swallow the gearstick."

Marcus finally shuts up, his lips forming a thin line as he exits the vehicle. Despite the nagging feeling I had to just uber home, I followed them in.

The music was ask expected, unnecessarily loud. There were far more people than I expected to be here, and that only made me even more agitated.

Marcus, Hanes and Gregory found four seats near the walls of the club, and claimed their territory there. They send for drinks, cigars, and dancers, while I leaned back in my chair.

"Michael, man," Gregory pats my leg, "I know you don't like this shit very much, but you gotta help us out, we're doing this for you,"

"If you were doing this for me, I'd be somewhere I actually want to be, not a fucking strip club."

"You're right," he raises both hands, "but we're here anyways, so . . . enjoy it?"

"Gregory please . . . shut the fuck up."

I wanted to disappear into my own world, one where my hands were dirty with mud and wet clay. One where my mind was at peace, focused, and occupied. One where sweat ripped from my forehead, the vibrant sounds of white noise as my background. But I couldn't do it if these grown men were going to keep pestering me all night.

"Ladies and Gentlemen, we have some very special guests here tonight," the host rings through the room, everyone coming to a halt as the music dies down.

"This . . . is what you've all been waiting for."

"Hell yeah!" Marcus screams and I let out an exasperated breath before inching away from him.

Five dancers with big feathers in their hair, strutted onto the stage, gathering everyone's attention. They all had the same outfits, just with different colors. Bling dazzled from their bellies to their thighs, heels ranging for 5 to 7 feet tall.

My eyes danced on all of them for a while, but stopped on the dancer with the tattoo running up her spine. She was the first to dance, her skin looked as smooth as butter, as clean as ice.

I tilted my head, my eyes following her every move. She was sensual, her dance steps teasing, drawling an almost invisible line between sexual and Dionysian.

Almost as if she could feel my eyes, in the blink of a second she was staring right back at me. I notice her miss a step, but she quickly plays it off. The dancer's eyes never leaves mine as she dances.

I look away, deciding that I wasn't doing myself a favor by eye-fucking anyone.

The night moves right along, and the only time I glanced at her was when she wasn't looking.

"Marcus, call her over," Hanes nudged Marcus, a glass of whiskey idle in his hands.

Marcus obviously accepts the challenge, being the twat he was. I watch as he speaks to one of the security guards, slipping money into his hands.

Soon enough, the security guard was escorting the woman I eye-fucked, and who eye-fucked me, over to Marcus's lap.

She strode over effortlessly, as if the heels that had her towering over us wasn't aching at her feet. We all looked up at her as she stood before us, a small, mischievous smile on her face. A small mask covered her eyes.

"Which one of you boys is Marcus?"

Marcus quickly raises his hands, Hanes and Gregory cheering him on as I turned to find the waitress. My throat felt dry.

As Marcus happily got his dance, I kept my eyes averted, observing the other dancers. They were good, but none were as good as her; in my opinion. I sneaked glances when I could, but after a while, it became unbearable. Marcus bathed in her attention, trying to slip ones into her creases and corners.

"Uh uh," she stops him, "you can tip me afterwards, I'm not a stripper."

"Sorry," he breathes, running a hand through his hair and she grins.

Finally having enough, I stand, moving to the bar section where I grab an orange juice. I find peace on the outside, where it was quiet. I knew I would be here for a while if I stuck with them, so I called up an uber, texted them I was leaving and left.

Like I said, this wasn't my scene, and it also isn't how I wanted to spend my last few minutes of my 26th birthday.

2. "THESE FUCKING BLACKS,"

"Hi, I'm looking to replace these but . . . I don't see them on the shelf,"

"Hey, great choice, the vanilla and cinnamon is such a nice fragrance, unfortunately we're out of stock."

Damn.

"I'm Hannah," she outstretches her hand and I take it.

"Noelle."

"Love your name," she gushes, her red hair swaying on her shoulders.

Vanilla and cinnamon was one of my best smells. I used it all the time before I danced. I felt like it did the job with attracting customers.

"We do have some similar fragrances if you'd like to check them out . . ."

"I kinda needed the Vanilla and Cinnamon, but I guess it won't hurt to just smell a few."

"Yay," she happily moved from around the counter, and down the 4th aisle.

"Here at Sincerely we take pride in creating different fragrances for our customers to enjoy, Mr. Kane is excellent at what he does."

"Oh, a man runs this company?"

"Yup, his formulas created all of these too, even the candles."

"Okay, wow. That's impressive."

She nods in agreement.

"This is our vanilla and coconut scent, our cocoa butter and cinnamon scent –,"

"I'd like to smell the cocoa butter one," the employee hands me the bottle and I spray it onto my fist, rubbing gently.

The smell was warm. It reminded me of fresh shower aftercare on a hot day. It reminded me of my mother hands, wrapping around my waist as she held me as I slept.

"I think as an addition I'll take this one."

"No pro –"

"So you're gonna steal it?"

Furrowing my eyebrows, I turn around to face a fat, hardly breathing white man staring down at me.

"Excuse me?"

"You said you're going to take the perfume. Does that mean you're going to steal it?"

Was this man on drugs?

"No," I answer simply, turning back to the employee who was as equally confused.

"Yes you did, I heard you say it," the man insisted.

"Sir, I'm rights here, how would she steal anything?" the employee asks and he scoffs.

"She'll do it right under your nose, you won't even notice," he says, "these fucking blacks."

"Woah," Hannah's widen at the same time that mine does.

"What the fuck did you just say?"

"It seems that you heard me, negro."

"Sir, you got five seconds to get your ass away from me before I wipe the floors with your titty sweat."

"Bitch you better watch how you talk to me."

He takes a step forward, successfully removing the space in-between us. I could feel his heat on my body, his nasty breath on my neck, it made my skin crawl.

Before I could stop it, my hands were swinging.

"No, no, no," Hannah sprinted away as I launched into the man, throwing cuffs into his face, "Mr. Kane! Mr. Kane!"

He was big, but he was too heavy to do much so I had a bit of an advantage.

"Get off me," he screams, "fucking monkey, get off –"

It was aggravating. The way I had his nose bleeding, his lips busted, and he was still hell bent on being racist. Maybe I hadn't done enough, maybe –

I'm being lifted off of him, strong hands resting right under my arm.

"Let go of me!"

I thrash in their grip as the drag me away.

After a second, they place me onto the floor. I turn around quickly, ready to give him their taste, but once I recognize him, I'm planted in place, just like on stage.

Recognition flashes in his eyes as well, and his lips part, his creased eyebrows now relaxed.

"It was him," I breathe, suddenly out of breath, "he was being racist – I -,"

"Call the cops!" He continues to wail in the background, a group of people surrounding him.

"Look, Y'all got cameras right? And I had an employee right next to me, he called me a monkey, he called me negro –"

"Breathe," the man in front me says, crossing his arms and I place a hand on my hip. Embarrassment glows on my cheek as I realize what I had done. I place a hand on my forehead, tears brimming my eyes.

"Shit," I whisper to myself.

"Relax," he repeats, "you're fine."

"I'm not fine, I just beat that man up."

"You said he was being racist," he shrugs, "sounds like he deserved it."

"I – but that only makes me – us what they say we are. Vile, angry, aggressive beings."

"Are you a just vile, angry, aggressive being, or were you provoked and as a result showed emotion?"

"I don't condone violence, especially not in my building," he places both of his hand behind his back, his chest slightly puffed as he tilts his head, "but I'll never tolerate discrimination or racism. Neither in here, nor out there. So believe me when I say that you're fine. Nothing will happen to you."

I let out a breath I didn't even know I was holding.

"I guess I should've given you the lap dance instead."

I expected him to laugh, maybe even smile, but he averted his eyes to the racist man.

"Hannah," he waves over one of his employees, "tell security to get that man's picture before throwing him out. He's banned from my store. Also, get her whatever she wants, I'll cover it."

"Yes sir," Hannah disappears and the man turns to leave.

"I apologize for the inconvenience, please accept my gifts."

"Wait!"

He pauses again, "er – do you know when these ill be back in stock?"

He merely tilts his head to look at the familiar bottle.

"It's the only scent I genuinely, wholeheartedly enjoy .."

"I don't know when they'll be back," he replies.

"Oh . . ."

The man takes this as his chance to leave, and I watch his back as he disappears.

He was . . . he was something and more.

3. "Are you really asking me out?"

R espectfully, Mr. Kane was fine.

I have never witnessed in my life a white man that made my knees go weak as he did. There was just something about him that attracted me that I couldn't put my finger on. He looked clean, that's for sure. His skin was flawless, not even a freckle. His hair was jet black, shiny and slightly faded on the sides. His body – oh my goodness – there's not much that I could see from his suit, but I knew that he was muscular. It wasn't anything drastic, because he also seemed a bit lean, but other than that, I just knew that man had abs.

Truthfully, every time this man looked at me, I felt like hands were wrapping around my neck. His eyes were so . . . blue. Despite what any book may depict, it is rather rare to see anyone with bright blue, or green eyes.

Mr. Kane hardly knew me, yet he had me standing in my mirror for ten minutes thinking about him.

I had taken a few things from the shop yesterday as 'gifts' and his candles were the truth. Long after they melted out, my room remained the smell of them. For three days now, my room has been smelling like honey and milk.

Also for three days now I've been buying candles and fragrances at his shop in hopes that I would see him. I met Hannah again, and she always apologized for the racist man's behavior but I was over that. All I wanted to do now was get to know her boss.

"Ooo, you look nice."

"Thanks, Cleo," I grin at my aunt clementine, who I lived with, and grabbed my keys off the table.

"Hot date?"

"Oh, how I wish," I reply honestly and she chuckles.

"Have a great day baby, and don't forget we're having later night dinner tomorrow!"

"You know I live here, right," I place a hand on my hip, "you could've reminded me tomorrow."

"Sometimes I forget," she lets out a cute, silly little laugh before returning to her laptop. She worked online as a virtual assistant and spent at least 12 hours a day on her computer.

I was dressed in a beige sundress, fashion slippers, and a nicely laid wig as I walked into Sincerely for the fifth time this week.

"Noelle," Hannah's smile blatantly displayed confusion.

"Hey," I greet. "I just can't get enough of any of these smells."

"Oh," she nods, letting out a breath of satisfaction, "yup, we get that a lot."

"Can I help you with anything today?"

"No, I think I'm alright, Hannah. I've got the place all mapped out."

"Alright," she chuckles, "enjoy the rest of your day."

I smile at her as she walks away before skipping towards the back where Mr. Kane's door was.

I eye it carefully, willing it to open, but like the other days, it never does. I walk around slowly, stopping at almost every perfume. By my thirtieth, my allergies were starting to kick in.

I decided that that was my cue to leave. A bit disappointed, I hardly notice the hunk of a man standing in the parking lot. He was speaking to the security card, his face as serious as ever.

"Okay, Noelle, this is your chance," I clear my throat quietly, before walking towards them, even if my car was in the opposite direction. I pretended to be looking for something in my bag as I near them, and they become quiet upon noticing me.

"Think I left my keys . . . " I murmur to myself, before letting out a loud exaggerated sigh. Turning to seem like I was heading back into the store.

"Oh – Mr. Kane," he shoves his hands in his pocket as he stares at me, "I didn't see you there."

"Howard, that'll be all." He dismisses the security guard and narrows his eyes at me for a moment before coming closer.

"I didn't get your name the other day."

"Noelle," I reply, and he nods.

"Noelle," he repeats, peering down at me with those icy blue eyes. "my security camera's recorded you here for the past five days. I guess you're enjoying my products."

"Uh – y-yeah, I am – definitely," I take a second to calm myself, humiliation creeping up my spine, "my room still smells like honey."

"Glad to hear it," he replies, "be sure to leave a review on our website."

"You've never told me your name," I blurt, and he leans on the car next to him.

"Yet, you seem to know it."

"Everyone here calls you Mr. Kane."

"I am Mr. Michael Kane," he says.

"Michael," I whisper to myself, and he rolls his lips into his mouth before taking a deep breath.

"It was nice seeing you again, Noelle. I should go in."

"No – wait!"

Damn it girl, relax.

"I was wondering if you'd like to go out with me?"

"Are you really asking me out?" For a moment, Michael smiles.

"Yeah," I shrug, "I see something that I like."

"I'm flattered, Noelle, really, but I have to be honest with you; I'm not – I don't want any extra relations right now. I'm focused on my business at the moment."

"Oh, well then, I guess we can settle to be friends?"

Michael chuckles slightly, "Thank you, you're a very . . . wonderful person. And I hope that you find your keys, if you need any help talk to security."

Michael nods at me one last time before leaving me in the parking lot, watching him walk away.

#

Now, who exactly did this man think he was?

I was confused. He seen all of this, and still said . . . no?

Maybe he just wasn't into black people, and that's fine, everyone has their preferences but I was into him so he should've made an exception.

"Noelle," my manager enters the room where I change, handing over a paperbag, "this is yours."

"Thanks, Mars," I push it into my bag, slipping on my flip-flops.

"Great job, as usual," she replies with a brief smile. We leave together, going our separate ways in the parking lot.

With burlesque dancing, there were good days, and then there were bad days. The bad days would be when the club is half empty, or when there's a fight and everyone has to leave early. I'd have to go home with hardly a night's worth of money in my pocket. The good days were a full house, tips that never ended, with respectful people. Tonight was a good day if you get what I mean. I had made at least eight hundred tonight, not including the tips I had stuck in my bra.

With my hand round the other seat, I happily drove home, Tink's Cap playing on my speakers. I vibed for the first ten minutes before I heard a loud noise coming from the back of my car.

I pull over on the side of the road, gaining the courage to go outside at almost two in the morning. The streets were pitch black with only the dull lampposts shedding a little light.

"No, no, no," I cried, as I watch my deflated tire. I had no spare, and it's highly unlikely that I'd get any tow truck or repairman out on the road at this time of night.

"Shit."

I wanted to call Aunt Cleo, but I knew she'd be in bed by now so that she could wake up for work tomorrow, and I didn't want to be inconsiderate.

But then what do I do? Do I sleep in the car? Do I walk home?

As a car speeds by, I realized what I had to do. With my thumbs out, my bag tightly wrapped under my hoodie, I stood on the side of the road, swallowing my pride.

I thought I'd be out here all night, God forbid that I get kidnapped.

A truck was the next vehicle that passed by, except it stopped for a moment.

"Where ya headed?"

From what I could see from the barely laminated road, I did not want to get in that truck.

"Oh – uh – I'm actually waiting on someone," I reply, "sorry about that?"

"Waiting on someone," the man chuckles, "miss your hands were outstretched towards the road. Are you stranded?"

"I – no – I already called someone, they're on their way."

"Are you sure? Would you like me to wait with you?"

To my dismay, he shuts off his engine.

"That's not necessary," I reassure him and he shrugs, opening his door.

"I insist. A lonely, beautiful girl out here in the dead of the night like this, all alone. It would simply be terrible of me to leave you out here."

"Sir I assure you that I'm fine, my boyfriend will be here any moment," I lie. I had an ill feeling in my stomach, my mouth dry as he walks towards me. This man easily towered over me, intimidating in both height and size. He had hair that was wrapped in a ponytail under his hat and a big ginger beard.

Gulping, I glance behind me to see if there was anywhere I could run, but getting lost in the forest didn't seem like a much better option.

"Boyfriend, huh," he reaches for me, and I yelp, jumping away.

"Leave me alone," panicked, I kick him between his legs. He doubles over, and I was about to take off running when headlights flash us.

By the time the owner of the new car approached us, I was having a full-on panic attack. My mind felt like it was closing in, my chest expanded and contracted with every desperate gasp for breath. I felt like my surroundings were all jumping out to me.

"Noelle," the new man whispers as he gently takes my hand. Out of reflex, I snatch it back roughly, colliding with the back of my vehicle.

"Breathe," he says. His scent was very familiar.

"No," I cry, tears pouring out of my eyes. I shut them, sliding down onto the ground.

"Noelle," he says more sternly, "breathe."

I try to breathe, but there just wasn't enough air.

"What the fuck did you do?" The man turns to my attacker who was watching the scene unfold in front of him. Next thing we knew he was climbing into his truck and speeding away.

As he left I felt cool, and I could feel the breeze passing through my finger, and underneath my thighs. My eyes focused on the blue eyes that peered into mine, and for some reason, I started crying even more. Michael places his hand around my hips, helping me off the ground, and carrying me into his vehicle. Whilst in the safety of his car, he waits quietly for me to calm down before he starts driving.

"I'm sorry," I tell him, using my jacket to wipe my now swollen eyes and runny nose.

"What're you sorry for, Noelle?"

"That must've been embarrassing for you,' I shake my head, "you probably have somewhere else to be as well, and I have you cooped up here."

"I'm heading home," he elaborates, leaning back in his chair. I noticed that he no longer had his blazer, nor his dress shirt on, instead, he had his undershirt that was still tucked into his slacks.

"You shouldn't be apologizing, that man attacked you."

I remain quiet. I'm not sure what that man's intention was, but it wasn't anything good. The entire situation felt surreal. It's like although you know that it can happen to you, that it can happen to anyone, you never really expect it to.

"Let's get you home then."

4. "JUST FOLLOW ME,"

The entire ride home was silent except for the few directions I would have to give him. I didn't know what to say, and it didn't seem like Michael had anything to say, so there was that.

"Do you live far from here?" I ask once we'd arrive at my house and he shakes his head.

"I live just on the hills," he says, pointing towards a little gated community in the distance and I nod.

"Okay, thanks again," I tell him, opening up my door to leave.

"Noelle," he calls right before I close the door. I poke my head into the car.

"I'd like to take your number if you don't mind, so I can check up on you."

"Oh, okay. Sure."

I put my digits into his phone, saving it as Noelle before handing it back to him.

"Thanks," he says, "are you alright?"

"I- I'm okay," he didn't look convinced but he didn't push it. I close the door before wrapping the hoodie tighter around me and disappearing into the house.

"Elle?"

In the darkness of my room, I hardly recognize my aunt standing in the doorway.

"Hey, did I wake you?"

"Oh no, I just about to head to bed."

"But it's late?"

"I know," she chuckles quietly, padding until she could sit on my bed, "I didn't hear your call pull in."

"Yeah," I sigh, "my tire popped."

"What? Why didn't you call me? How'd you get home?"

"Uh - a f-friend of mine . . .I didn't want to wake you."

"Nonsense," she scoffs, "Noelle whenever you're in trouble I need you to promise that you'll call me. I don't know what I would do if something happened to you a-and I wasn't there to help or stop it."

"Okay," I whisper, thankful that she didn't turn on any lights, because the tears were making a reappearance.

"Life is unpredictable, and with the work that you do, I know you'll often come home late. So believe me when I say that I won't think twice if you call me because you're in danger, or because your tire runs flat. I love you, Noelle . . . . I . . . I consider you to be my daughter, so it's my job to protect you . . . even as you're a bit older now."

"Thank you, Aunt Cleo," my voice was shaky, and I anxiously pulled at the skin in my palms, "I love you too."

"Your mother would be so happy to see you right now, a grown woman, doing her thing, making her money, staying out of trouble. You're amazing, Elle, and I need you to remember that, even on your bad days. Even when you're away from home, just remember that this, here, will always be your home."

"Cleo," I breathe, taking her hand in mine, "where's this coming from?"

She takes a deep breath before shaking her head, her pink bonnet stiff despite her movements.

"Everyone needs reassurance now and then, Noelle, I'm just making sure that you have yours." She plants a kiss on my forehead, rubbing my shoulders.

"Sleep tight."

"You too," she shuts the door gently behind her, and the moment she does I burst into tears.

What happened tonight was . . . traumatizing. Every time I closed my eyes I saw his face. It was filled with bad intentions. I was so vulnerable, what if Michael hadn't shown up? Would I be dead? Stuffed in the woods like a roadkill animal? Would I be tied up at the back of his truck?

The worst part is, there was no one to blame. I . . . I was the one that put myself in that situation, I was on the street, at two am, hitchhiking because I hadn't check my tire.

It was . . . it was my fault.

#

The next morning, I woke up to continuous beeps in my driveway. I felt like I was hungover.

"Noelle? Noelle, honey, did you get your car fixed and towed?"

Aunt Cleo knocked on my door. Knowing damn well I hadn't done anything to fix the car situation, I jumped out of bed almost knocking into the floor, and peeped into my window.

Sure enough, there was my car, back in my driveway looking pretty much brand new. I had a dent in the back that had mysteriously gone away, and an entirely new paint job and shine.

Aunt Cleo waited outside my door, and when she saw me she gave me a confused look.

"Uh – it must be my friend," I tell her before racing down the stairs.

"Damn, your friend must have money then," she replies behind me and I let out a nervous laugh.

The tow truck made me sign, and when I asked who told them my address they confirmed that it was Michael.

He had completely fixed my car.

"Wow," Cleo folded her arms as she stood in front of my car with me, "are you sure they didn't just buy you a new one?"

"I . . . I – don't you have to get ready for work?"

She narrows her eyes at me, folding her arms over her Versace robe.

"Let me find out that you got a man, little girl," she jokes and I roll my eyes.

"Tell your boss I'd like a Versace robe as well."

"Hey! Don't think you're too old to get whopped," Aunt Cleo laughed all the way into the house and I couldn't help but smile at her retreated figure.

Looking back at the car, I saw my reflection and immediately felt depressed. My eyes were puffy, not all that red, and my face look swollen. I wondered if Aunt Cleo noticed.

Once back in my room, I grabbed my phone and found that Michael had called and texted me. It was an unknown number, but I knew it was him.

Michael: I don't usually send texts but you didn't answer. Maybe you're asleep . . . or maybe you've seen the car in your driveway. Whatever it is, just know that I took care of it; the bill and all, so you don't have to worry. I'd like you to be safe, so you should be alright from now. Have a good day, ~ Mr. Kane.

I see why he preferred calls, he typed like he was writing a letter. Hell, he should've just sent me an email.

Regardless, his message put a smile on my face so early in the morning. I couldn't repay him, at least not the price of all the repairs because I'd have to empty my savings; I hardly ever saved. Maybe when Cleo forced me to.

But maybe I could treat him to lunch, and there's no way I'll take no for an answer.

\#

My face was still puffy, even after I steamed and rolled it. I wore a bit more makeup today in hopes that it'll hide it.

I threw on one of my two-piece sets. A cami crop top and maxi high slit skirt with some glass slipper heels. My hair, my wig, was pulled into a ponytail.

When I arrived at Sincerely, Hannah was nowhere to be seen, and I was glad. The last thing I needed was her seeing me asking out her boss for the second time, and probably getting rejected.

"Hi," I approach the security guard, a polite smile on my face, "how can I get to Mr. Kane?"

"Good day, do you have an appointment with him?"

"Uh – no – I'm a friend of his and –"

"You can't just walk up and see Mr. Kane," he says, his tone bland, "you're not asking to see an employee, you're asking to see the boss, a very important man –"

"Howard, it's alright," Michael appears out of nowhere his hands patting at his jeans.

I noticed he wasn't in his formal wear, instead, he wore jeans and a T-shirt . . . and Nike slides.

I was definitely overdressed.

He rests his hands on the upper part of my arm, leading me outside.

"I just wanted to say thanks – in person – for completely taking care of my care. You didn't have to do that."

"You're welcome," he nods, shoving his hands in his pockets.

"And . . . I'm going to take you out to lunch for it."

"Noelle –,"

"It isn't a date, Michael," I tilt my head at him, "it's just payment."

"If you wanted to pay me back you'd have to take me to lunch at least four times, every day for three years."

"Oh, okay – wow," my eyes widen.

"It's okay, Noelle," he chuckles, "I'm actually busy -,"

"If you don't let me take you out to lunch, I'll stand in your store all day."

"It's a free country."

"I'll destroy your products."

"I'll have you arrested, and sue you."

"Come on, Michael," I let out an exasperated sigh, "is the thought of having lunch with me that horrendous? Just give me an hour, it'll help soothe my conscience."

Michael seemed conflicted. His eyes darkened, and his lips moved from side to side.

"Alright, fine. An hour."

"Great," I clap and he shakes his head at me, "I'll drive."

"No, we'll both drive. Just in case I'd like to escape," Michael dusts off his hands, "give me a moment, I need to wash off my hands."

As Michael disappears into Sincerely, and I did a little dance in the parking lot before calming myself.

He returns a few minutes later with another T-shirt.

"Where're we going?

"Um, where do you normally eat?"

"At home."

"Oh – okay well . . . I could eat a sub right now, wanna go to Subway?"

He shrugs, "I'm being forced so I don't think it matters."

"Oh my goodness," I roll my eyes at him, "just follow me."

5. "True Story,"

M ICHAEL'S POV

Noelle dragged me all the way across town to grab Subs at Subway. We literally passed four branches on the way.

"This one just tastes better," she explains once we arrive.

I didn't even know why I had given in to her peer pressure, but it was something about her being so persistent that made me curious. What did this woman really want with me?

She was adorable though, I watched as her eyes went wide looking at all of the toppings, and they went even wider when she saw the cookies.

"Okay, okay, okay," she breathes as her turn comes up, "hi, can I have ham sub with no olives please, lots of dressing, and three double chocolate cookies."

"Sure, and what about you?"

"Just get me a meatball sub," I reply and she nods. Noelle turns to stare at me, giving me a weird look.

"You don't want a cookie?"

"No."

"Why?"

"I don't need one,"

"No one ever needs a cookie," she rolls her eyes and I purse my lips, "fine, I'll give you one of mine."

When our orders were done, she drags me to a table, and –

"You have about 32 minutes left with me –"

"Do you have a girlfriend, Michael?"

"I don't," unwrapping my sub, I avoid her eyes as she tries to figure me out.

"A boyfriend?"

I purse my lips even further, regretting my decision to join her even more.

"Alright, a situationship ? A complicated –"

"I don't have anything, nor anyone," I state briskly, increasingly getting irritated.

"So you just don't like . . . me?"

I shrug, "it's not that I don't like you, I think you're an interesting person, a bit controlling but interesting. And you're very . . . beautiful . . . but I'm just not looking for anyone right now."

"I understand," she says, nodding and I take a bite into my sub.

"you've been hurt before then," she asks softly, "I don't mean to pry . . . just making conversation."

"It's fine, and no, I haven't really. I've pretty much had one relationship in my entire life and we both agreed that it would be best to just end it. After that, I focused on my business, my art, and found that life doesn't need anyone else to feel complete."

"Really," she raises an eyebrow, "you found all that out after one relationship."

"True story" she chuckles, shaking her head at me and I tilt mine at hers.

"Alright then, Mr. loner boy, I get it then, you're simply not looking for any extra relations right now."

We eat in silence for just a few seconds, and just as I was starting to enjoy it, she started talking again.

"Did you enjoy the show?"

"by the show, do you mean watching you?"

Noelle smirks, leaning forward on the table.

"So you were watching me?"

I didn't want to play her game, she was baiting me. Clever, but just not clever enough.

"I have to admit, I was watching you. I looked at every inch of skin you left uncovered, every curve, and with every move you made, I felt like you were dancing only for me," I smirk as her lips part, leaning back in my chair, "and even after all that, I still didn't go on a date with you."

Her mouth drops open.

"That's just so mean," she chuckles, and I can't help but smile.

It was a surprise that she didn't take my comment to heart, and I was impressed because now she had me chuckling and smiling with her.

"You know I've been in probably . . . two relationships my entire life and I've never been the one to approach them . . . or anyone matter –of – fact."

"What happened to your previous relationships?"

"One cheated on me . . . with my previous boss, and the other just . . .left."

"Hmm, I'm sorry to hear that."

"No, it's okay it's - it's in the past."

"Did you love them?"

Noelle ponders on it for a moment, looking down at her cookie.

"I did," she slowly fondles with it, her mood seemingly changing.

"Then it's their loss."

She looks up quickly, tilting her head at me.

"Seeing how persistent you were with me, taking me out to lunch and buying me a $10 sub to repay me for the ten thousand dollars I spent on you today, I can tell you're a huge catch."

She bows, a smile gracing her face, "I'm the best fish out there."

"Are those good?" I nod towards her cookies, and she slides over one for me.

"Have one yourself."

The cookie looked pretty cookieish. It was round and soft, with almost the perfect texture. I twisted it in my hand, Noelle waiting on me to shove it into my mouth.

I thought about the quality of the cookie, it looked really good.

"Michael . . . it's a cookie, not a diamond."

"Sorry to keep you waiting, Madam," I take a bite, resisting the urge to groan as the chocolate melts in my mouth.

"This is good," I reply with a nod, and her grin is wide. She pumps her hand into her hair to mimic triumph.

We eat the cookies in silence and end up ordering a few more. Before I knew it, an hour turned into two, but I wasn't ready to leave. Noelle was perfect company. She was a little out of my pick, because of how extroverted she could be, but I think . . . I think she compliments me quite well.

"Everyone is so afraid of commitment these days . . . it's disappointing. I would never get into an open relationship – I mean I'm not bashing anyone who does, but it just isn\t for me. I want . . . unconditional love . . . I want the problems that come with it, and the genuineness of our love . . . but I do understand. As someone who has been hurt before there's a fear of getting into a new relationship because you're never entirely sure who that person is."

"Yet you still believe in love."

"Because love is something that we all need. Love is . . . love is everything. And despite what we may think after being repeatedly hurt not everyone is the same . . . people come into your lives for different reasons so honestly, I think it's just . . . all part of the plan."

When she said it that way, it made sense. All she was really trying to say is that one relationship doesn't define the rest of your relationships. I didn't know very much about them though, I was in one relationship throughout my entire life and well it ended because I believe that we were both very bland.

"That's a very good outlook on it."

Noelle smiles in response, gathering her trash neatly. She was as pretty as a picture, sitting across from me. I didn't want to get involved with her, because I'm focused on myself. I'm focused on building my future. I didn't come from wealth, I created it myself and I had to work twice as hard as anyone who had the money handed to them. Not only the childhood friends that I had were either committed or married and still found leisure time to entertain strippers and spend nights in hotel rooms.

"Alright . . . well, I think we're done," she says, and surprisingly, I felt disappointed.

"I held you long enough," she chuckles, standing from her seat, and I do the same. She takes her trash and mine and throws it out.

We step outside into the streets and stare at our vehicles.

"So, I paid you back," Noelle nods, dangling her keys in her hands, "I guess I'll see you around, Michael."

"Yeah," I mutter and she offers me one last smile before walking over to her vehicle.

"Uh – Noelle," I call right before she gets in. She pauses, half of her body already in.

"Is that date still on the table?"

6. "I Love That For You,"

"**N**o, it isn't," I told him, and it was hilarious the way his face contorted into one of confusion.

"Well then," he shoves his hand in his pockets, rocking back on his heels, "I suppose that's fair."

Rolling my eyes, I place a hand on my hip, "I'm kidding."

Michael's face goes flat, his lips forming a thin line.

"Just text me with the time and place," I blow him a kiss, using his silence as an opportunity to climb into my vehicle, and drive home.

Aunt Clementine sat at her desk in the living room, pushing her glasses up from her nose.

We wave at eachother since her headset was on, and she point at the kitchen. I shake my head indicating that I wasn't hungry.

Now in the comfort of my room, I turned on the A/C and dived under the comfort of my sheets. There wasn't much to do during the day, so when curiosity called, I gladly answered.

Michael Kane.

Google results popped up 0.71seconds later, and unsurprisingly, there wasn't very much about him. I mean there were lots of speculating articles, lots of pictures, but there was nothing personal.

This was expected, Michael seemed like a very private person, and not only that but he doesn't speak very much.

Michael Kane refuses to interview with FAME Magazine.

Billionaire Michael Kane, says NO to CNN interview

Michael Kane has NO WORDS on the growing success of his fragrance line.

The titles were all pretty much the same, and so I didn't look into them very much. The pictures of him were all taken by reporters and it usually seemed like he had no idea his pictures were being taken.

Knowing that there wouldn't be any social media accounts for him, I didn't even bother looking.

"Elle," Cleo calls from the door.

"Come in," I yell, sitting up in bed, and the door slowly creeks open, "are you on lunch?"

"Yeah, it's a bit late but we had a bunch of work to get done today," she places her hands on her hips, "did you eat out?"

"I did actually . . . with a friend."

"Oh," she lets out a little laugh that resembled one of a French chef, and looked at me side-eyed, "you're gonna sit with me at lunch, and we're going to talk about this friend."

"What if it was a girl?"

"Thank you for telling me that it's not," she winks, turning to leave, "I'm waiting!"

I couldn't help but laugh. I got up though, padding into the living room and lifting myself up onto the kitchen counter as she warmed up her food.

"So who's this lucky man?"

"Aunt Cleo, I said I had lunch with the man, not that I married him."

"Nevertheless, anyone who's in the presence of my niece is extremely lucky."

Aunt Cleo leaned against the counter as the microwave hummed and I hid my smile looking down at my swinging feet.

"His name is Michael . . . Michael Kane," I tell her.

"Michael Kane," she repeats, her eyes locked onto the ceiling. She folded an arm, a finger on her chin.

"He sounds very familiar."

"He owns the fragrance and candle store, Sincerely."

"Oh wow," she lets out a breath, nodding, "that's very impressive."

"Right?" I fangirl.

"What is he like? Do you like him?"

I hesitate on telling her that I had a date with him coming up, but I give in anyway because this was Aunt Cleo. The woman who's raised me since I was sixteen years old, and made me feel nothing but loved, accepted, and appreciated since then. We shared everything.

"He's . . . quiet," I state, biting the inside of my cheek, "but he's very respectful. There are no red flags, he tells me what it is, and then we go from there. He's a great listener, and . . . we laugh . . . a lot. We . . . also plan to go on a date."

"I love that for you," she gushes earnestly, placing a firm hand on my arm, "you better go ahead and seek that type of happiness."

"And when will you do the same?"

Clementine rolls her eyes, a small smile on her face. She turns towards her food, passing a fork through it.

"You know damn well there's a connection between the two of you, that man adores you."

"That man is also my boss," she emphasizes.

"Yet he sends you designer items, gives you extra benefits, and don't forget he paid off the house."

"Because I'm a great assistant."

"You're in denial," I tilt my head at her as she walks around me and grabs her unsweetened grapefruit juice from the fridge.

Aunt Cleo sighs, "Even if I did, Ella, he lives an entire flight away."

"I'm sure that the two of you can come up with some type of arrangement, you're making excuses."

"Alright, young lady," she shakes her head, "we're here to talk about your love life, not mine."

"I wouldn't call it a love life just yet."

I stepped down from the counter, as Aunt Cleo makes herself comfortable in the living room.

"I'm gonna sort some outfits for tonight."

"Okay sweetheart, I can't wait to see how you look."

Before I went back to my room, I just stood and stared at her. I didn't mean to be creepy, but I've been a burlesque dancer for three years now, I work almost 6 nights a week, every month, and each time Clementine wants to see how I look.

If she could, she would add any jewels she had hanging around in her room, or she would recommend another stocking or top, and then she would call me perfect.

My parents were great, but Aunt Cleo was wonderful.

She didn't ask for me as a responsibility, but she stepped up and she did a damn good job. I loved her so much, I just hoped she knew that she was amazing. I hoped she knew that I could take care of myself now, and it's time for her to go ahead and seek her happiness.

#

A few minutes before I left for work, my phone lit up with a call.

My heart raced in my chest as Michael's name displays across the screen. I take a deep breath, tapping accept and raising the phone to my ear.

"H-hey," I stammered, swallowing hard.

"Hey." Michael's voice was husky, and a bit harsh. He was seemingly breathless.

"Are you alright?" I furrow my eyebrows in confusion.

"Oh yeah," he chuckles, "just got done with a workout, I thought I'd give you a call about our date."

"Oh – uh – yeah, totally, what's up?"

"I know you work at night, so I was wondering if breakfast would be okay for you?"

"Yes, that's perfectly fine."

"I usually have my breakfast at six, but I'll make an exception for you tomorrow."

"Why, thank you, kind sir," I tease, idly walking in circles.

"Most welcome, I'll pick you up at nine."

"It's a date."

"It is."

We hang up and although our conversation was short, and to the point, I could stop smiling. I could almost see what he looked like shirtless, and sweating, lips parted as he breathed. The man was just so hot.

Not only that but just hearing his voice made me go all tingly inside. I wanted to melt.

To say that I was excited about tomorrow was an understatement, and it was a relief that our date would be in the morning, so I wouldn't have to wait too long.

Felling this way even before the first day had to be illegal, and if I wasn't careful, I would end up falling on my ass.

7. "see, I was just Hungry,"

The next morning was particularly colder, and it rained a bit. I silently prayed that this wouldn't ruin the date. I had woken up at the crack of dawn, barely having slept at all, just filled with excitement.

I wanted to go with a loose outfit today, that showed a bit of skin but still left to the imagination. I went with a dress that sat just above my knee, it was yellow, giving brunch vibes, and had little ruffles at the end. The chest area had a deep plunge and the waist stuck to me like a glove.

I paired the dress with wedge heels and a woven bag.

I wasn't a fan of very heavy makeup but I did enjoy a few enhancers so I threw on some lashes, lip liner, lipgloss, and base makeup.

By the time it was nine, I was pacing my room nervously. My stomach felt like a bottomless pit, and my hands were sweaty.

"Noelle?" Aunt Cleo pops her head into the room, "a Michael is here for you."

She smirks knowingly and I playfully narrow my eyes at her, before gathering myself.

"You look amazing," she whispers, nodding in approval as she strolled behind me.

"Thank you," I grin, before regaining my composure and joining him in the living room.

Michael's hands were as usual, buried in his pockets.

If it's one thing I adored, it was a man that was secure in his masculinity. So secure that wearing neatly ironed pink pastel-colored slacks, didn't bother him. In fact, they looked like they were made for him. He paired it with a light blue button-up and white button-up, and a baby blue blazer. Everything fit him so well, I wouldn't be surprised if he had it made for him.

"Noelle," his eyes skimmed all over me, and I nervously hold the bag with both hands in front of me, "there isn't a word I could possibly use to describe how ... beautiful ... alluring ... enthralling you look."

"I think you named a few," I titter, and he smiles.

"This is for you," he outstretches a bouquet towards me, and with my lips parted, I take them from his hands.

"Thank you," I beamed.

He raises his head to nod at Aunt Cleo who sat in the background. She tried not to look suspicious, but it was obvious that her headphones weren't all the way around her ears.

"Shall we?"

He steps aside to allow me to walk in front of him and I look back at Clementine, give him a small, yet exciting wave to which she replies with two thumbs up.

"You clean up very nicely as well," I compliment him as he opens up the door for me and he raises an eyebrow.

"It's okay," he tilts his head, "you can call me beautiful."

"Alright, Shakespeare," I snicker and he narrows his eyes at me, climbing into the driver's side.

"I miss the Michael that I left with my aunt."

#

Michael took me to Skyliner's. It was a very prestigious and costly restaurant, that had amazing seats right at the top. It opened up to the morning sky, but we decided to dine indoors since the rain would make the experience unpleasant.

"What your step," Michael instantly takes my hand as we approach the stairs, helping me up since I wore heels. I quietly wondered if he felt how sweaty my palms were, but if he did, he didn't seem to be bothered by it.

He didn't let go of my hand as we approached the receptionist, and although I was cheesing inside, I remain as cool and collected as I could, pretending as if I had done this many times before.

"Good morning," she smiles at the both of us, "hope you two are having a wonderful morning –"

"I made a reservation for two. It's under the name Michael Kane."

"Oh, alright," she lets out an awkward laugh before nodding, "we have you right here at table four, follow me."

She leads us to our table, and Michael pulls the seat out for me, before pushing the chair gently into the table. The receptionist lets us know that our waitress will be with us shortly.

"This place is legit," I mutter, shifting to get comfy in the chairs.

"It is, I haven't been here very often though, maybe once or twice for business meetings."

"Is the food good?"

"From the little I've tasted, it is."

The waitress approaches our table, a warm smile on her face. The atmosphere here was absolutely welcoming.

"Hi, welcome to Skyliners. I'm Macy, and I'll be your waitress for the night."

I offer her an encouraging smile as she sets down the menus, her fingers shaky.

"I'll give you a moment to browse through the menu, and I'll be back."

"Thanks," Micahel murmurs, taking his into his hands.

We sat in silence for a few seconds.

"Does anything look good to you?" He asks and I hum indecisively.

"The chocolate chip oatmeal is really sticking out to me . . . and maybe the omelette. What do you think?"

"I was thinking the omelette as well, and some fruit."

"That's it?"

"They're serving proportions are fairly large."

"Well, in that case, I think we're ready."

We end up flagging the waitress because she hadn't returned yet.

"Wow, you guys are the most decisive people we've ever encountered," she chuckles, "most people take –"

"She'll have the chocolate chip oatmeal, and an omelette, and I'll have an omelette as well with a fruit bowl."

My mouth dropped open as Michael disregards the waitresses' small talk, leaving her standing there with red cheeks.

"Do you want anything to drink?" He asks me.

"I'll have the freshly squeezed orange juice please."

"Just water for me."

"G-got it. Your order will be right up." She quickly disappears, leaving me to stare at Michael.

"What?"

"That was very impolite," I scold and leans back in his chair.

"Her job is to collect our order and bring the food. Not make conversation."

"I get that but cutting her off is . . . rude . . . I'm sure she feels embarrassed."

"I usually eat at six," he reminds me, "I haven't eaten all morning and I'm not trying to be crappy, but she should maintain professionalism. What if she waiting on me to take the order, and I held her back by talking about how many other waiters don't wait for me properly. Her first comment was accepted, but she wanted to go on and on."

"So . . . you're going to cut me off every time I talk about something that isn't important to you or isn't convenient for you?"

Michael remains quiet, his face neutral, "I wouldn't do that to you."

The date was off to an awkward start, and it irritated me a little that he was so rude to the waitress. She was just trying to be polite and although I understand his standpoint I think that it's important that he learns to acknowledge other's feelings and not just his at the moment.

The waistress returns with our food in less than fifteen minutes.

"Omelette, Oatmeal, and Orange juice for you, and Omelette, fruit bowl, and water for you."

"Thank you," I smiled, and she hesitantly smiles back.

"Macy," Michael reaches into his pocket, "I apologize for rudely interrupting –"

"Oh no," she exclaims, "it's. I – I understand."

He pulls out a hundred-dollar bill and hands it to her. Her eyes were wide.

"Nevertheless, take this as a tip."

Macy reluctantly takes the money from his fingertips.

"Thank you so much," she nods "I really do appreciate it. Please, enjoy your meal."

She leaves us alone, and I can't help but crack at a smile at him.

"See," he shrugs, " I was just hungry."

8. "Say Sike Right Now,"

The rest of the date went smoothly after that. The fact that Michael apologized and tried to reconcile after I expressed that I didn't appreciate the way he interacted with the waitress, made me really happy. He didn't apologize to me either, he apologized to HER, and that's the most important thing.

The food here was flavorsome. The chocolate chip oatmeal really got me because they cooked it up so well. It was bland prison food, it was sweet, and filled with spices, and the chocolate only made it taste like one of those subway cookies that I adored.

"It's that good, huh?"

"It's amazing, I almost forgot that I was on a date," Michael seemed to enjoy watching me eat because he barely ever took his eyes off me.

"How's your omelette?"

"Fluffy. I don't particularly like the ham but other than that I'd give it a nine on ten."

"Awesome," I place another spoonful into my mouth before taking another casual glance around.

"You really do look beautiful, Noelle, I . . . I can't stop looking at you."

"Michael, if you keep this up my cheeks will start hurting," I rolled my lips into my mouth.

"It's true," he insists, and I sigh.

"Than –"

"Don't thank me, beautiful, this is all you."

"This is crazy," I breathe, "I mean am I dreaming or something? Say sike right now."

We both laugh, and I push my plate aside, feeling full.

"Just a few days ago you barely even wanted to have platonic lunch with me."

"I know," he hums, "if I'm being honest I didn't see dating in my near future. But you were so persistent to lunch . . . and then we had an actual conversation . . . and then you made me laugh . . . like genuinely laugh and I don't know, I just wanna see where this will go."

"I completely understand," I bubbled, "but what're we talking about this fine morning, I've never really done anything like this."

"You've been in two relationships."

"I told you how they ended though, so you should've had an idea of how they went overall."

Michael chuckles, rubbing under his chin.

"Alright um, tell me about your family, you live with your aunt?"

"I do. I have been since I was fifteen actually."

"Oh . . . then If you don't mind me asking, where're your parents?"

I take a deep breath, idly itching my eyebrow, "they're dead."

"Oh shit," he shut his eyes momentarily, "I'm sorry –"

"No stop, what're you apologizing for? It's okay."

"I don't mean to pry and if anything makes you uncomfortable feel free to let me know."

"You're a sweetheart, Michael, and it's completely fine. I think I've just come to terms with their death. They were in the army so."

"But," I raise a finger, "they did leave me in the hands of the best woman on Earth, so I'm actually not all that mad at them."

"Your aunt? She does seem pretty nice. She has a very warm voice."

"She does," I agree, "what about your family?"

"Um," he leans back in his chair again, scratching the back of his neck, "my mom's a hairstylist, my dad's a farmer and I have two sisters that's in college right now. It's all just pretty . . . usual."

"You're right, I'm not sure what I was expecting to hear but it wasn't that."

"Why not?"

"because you're . . . you know . . ."

"Successful?"

"Extremely wealthy."

"Ahh," he nods, "I get that. A lot of people assume that my wealth was generational or that I had some sort of huge advantage that brought me where I am today but that couldn't be farther from the truth. I got here off of pure hard work and talent. One minute I'm in my basement experiment with different smells that I enjoy, the next minute my mother's selling fragrances for me to her neighbors and friends."

"And it was only up from there."

"I can't blame them, your scents are unique, and they last forever. Not to mention they contain no harmful chemicals that're too harsh for the skin. If you made a lotion line, I would personally buy you out."

Michael cackles, throwing his head back in genuine laughter. I giggle at the sight.

"I guess that's something I'll have to consider," he added, "I feel like we're talking about me a little too much. Let's see what's going on with you."

He narrows his eyes playfully, tapping a finger on his chin, "how'd you get into dancing?"

"A friend of mine introduced me to it. I couldn't find a job and they were hiring so I just had to get with the program. No cute, inspirational backstory there."

"You're good at it though," he shrugs, "I think that in itself is the inspiration."

"It's the black in me, I love to dance - in fact I love anything that requires rhythm."

"I can't dance to save my life. I'll look like a scooting dog."

I cover my mouth with a palm, my eyes wide as I hold in my laughter.

"Now, Michael, why would you say that?" I chortle and he grins.

"I'm being honest here, don't laugh."

He places his hands on the table, stretching it to where mine was. I don't move, anticipating his touch.

Finally, his hands enclose mine, and my heartbeat accelerates at the feeling of his soft, firm hands around mine.

I let out a little nervous giggle, looking up at him. He was already looking at me though, his eyes boring into mine.

"Um, burlesque dancing i-is fun. The glitters, and the jewels, the empowering feeling, it's all very encouraging. But like everything it has it's . . . cons. People often mistake us for strippers, and they try to get handsy . . . or disrespectful. Sometimes it can get overwhelming but we have personal security that comes to our rescue. The attention can be nice but there are boundaries, you know?" he nods.

"After a while, you learn to deal with it," I look down at my bag on my lap, basking in the feeling of Michael's thumb rubbing against my hand.

"Alright, that was depressing," I joke, "we can talk about something else."

"It's not, don't do that. I want you to express yourself freely with me, I'm always listening."

"This is our first date, Michael, you're starting to seem too good to be true," I lean forward, licking my lips and he sheepishly smiles.

"My bad, I'll dial it down a little."

"What're your future goals? What do you look forward to the most?"

He ponders on it for a second, "I don't know . . . I feel like I'm comfortable with where I am, and what I'm doing currently. As for the future, what's supposed to happen will happen, I've learned not to waste now by thinking about later."

I smile briefly at his answer, looking down at the table cloth, before gingerly looking back up at him.

"I earnestly wish I could say the same. That I wasn't worried about my future but I . . . I feel like we're. . . like I'm in this endless loop. Like life just goes on and on and there's just no meaning for it. I feel like there just has to be something more than this and if there isn't . . . I'm not sure that I'd like to live like this for the rest of my life – I'm sorry, was that depressing again –"

"Noelle," he calls, in a firm, scolding tone, "your feelings are valid - your emotions are valid. I'm serious. Stop apologizing for sharing what's on your mind."

"And although I've never stopped to think about it . . . that actually makes a lot of sense."

Michael's phone rings to life, and he glances at it. His eyebrows raise slightly, and he lets out a small grunt.

"It's twelve already," he taps a few times before looking up at me, apologetically.

"You've got to go," I slouch, averting my eyes to hide the disappointment.

"I'm sorry," he says softly, "I have a meeting, I would reschedule but it's important."

"No, it's fine. I'm pretty sure first dates don't last three hours anyway," I shake my head whilst putting my stuff together.

He flags over the waitress who brings the bill, and pays it off.

Once again, he takes my hand to help me down the stairs, and opens up the passenger side for me.

"Mr. Kane," a man with a camera quickly runs up to him, and I watch as his face becomes ice cold, "Mr. Kane are you dating? Mr. Kane can you tell The Montage if that woman in the passenger seat is your significant other?"

"No, but I can tell you to fuck off," he spits, swiftly sliding into the driver side, and pulling out.

"You're a celebrity around here, huh?"

"I wouldn't say that," he huffs, shifting in his seat, "the problem is I won't give them what they want, and when someone can't get what they want . . ."

"Well, what do they want?"

"An invitation into my life."

9. "NOELLE!"

As I watched Michael drive from the side of my eye, I tried to memorize the features on his face. He was truly a beautiful man. His intricate jaw line, the small marks left on the sides of the bridge of his nose from his classes, the 5 o'clock shadow that perhaps he forgot to shave - or maybe . . . he liked it like that. I know I did.

Shit, overall aura did more than enhance his fuckableness. Excuse my French.

He looked so lost as he drove though, I wondered where he was. I clear my throat, and he blinks a few times before glancing at me.

"You alright?"

"I'm fine," I reply, tilting my head at him, "although . . . I should be asking you."

He chuckles, shaking his head, "I'm okay. I was just thinking about a second date for you and I."

My lips part as I stare at him, and he smirks, obviously knowing the effect he had on me.

"Sheesh," I grin, "A second date? And I didn't even have to beg this time."

Michael rolls his eyes, "I must admit that I'm glad you didn't give up . . . I would've missed out on all of this."

I sink further into my chair, smiling in content.

"What were you thinking of doing?"

"I don't know, you work pretty late so there's not much night life we could cover, maybe a late afternoon movie?"

"Oh," I nod, "I actually haven't been to the movies in years."

"Me too," he replies, "it's settled then, tomorrow at 4?"

"Yes, I will text you the schedule."

"Sounds like a plan."

He drove me all the way home, even stepping out to pull open my door, and walk me to the house.

"You know, you're a sweetheart when you aren't being a mutt," I joke, and he presses his lips in a thin line.

"I'm just going to ignore the last part and say, thank you."

I giggle, looking down at my shoes.

He takes my chin, lifting my head so that I could look at him, "later?"

"Later," I breath, my heart accelerating in my chest. My eyes drop to his lips, and for a moment I thought he was going to kiss me.

He swerves, placing a gentle kiss on my cheek before stepping away.

"Call me after work, please," he says as he walks away.

"I will," I mutter, mostly to myself. I watch confusedly as he leaves, before turning to push the door open nearly tripping over the step.

I watch as he drives off, giving a small wave before pushing the front door open.

My aunt sat in her usual corner, her headphones wrapped around her head but her eyes set on me. She raises her eyebrows and tilts her head and I already knew what that meant; after work, I'd be her target.

I roll my eyes teasingly, but nod nevertheless.

I had a bit of time before work as it was only one in the afternoon, so I decided to binge some shows, and take a nap.

\#

Tonight was packed.

I wasn't complaining because that meant a bigger share of money for us, but for a Thursday evening it was a bit alarming.

The girls and I did what we do best: dance. And of course, the crowd loved us. A few newcomers tried to throw money at the stage but our security had to let them know that they were in the wrong club.

I spend at least an hour on the stage with the other girls, and by the time I was done, my calves were aching, and my mouth was dry.

"Is it just me or was the club swamped?"

"It was," I confirm, stretching out my legs, "if today was swamped, I can just imagine tomorrow."

Mia groans, leaning back onto the wall. The girls walk around us, all rubbing at their joints.

"Do you every just . . . not want to do this anymore?"

I pause for a moment.

In all honesty, after I got this job, I never really thought about doing anything else.

Its like you're a fish, swimming in water, and you're so tired of swimming but it's become so normal, that you never actually think about getting out of the water.

I mean – the fish would die, but you get what I'm saying here.

"Actually . . . I don't think I've actually ever thought of doing something else."

"Hm," she shakes her head, "then you're strong. I personally don't know how long I'll last here."

Mia stands, grabbing her bag to go into the shower room and I'm left wondering what I would do if I didn't have this job.

My phone vibrates in my bag, breaking me out of my trance.

Michael: Noelle, have you left work yet?

If I had never met Michael in person and he texted me, I would overthink every text he sent. Because why did he start off with my first name instead of a greeting like a normal human being?

Noelle: No, I'm actually about to leave.

Michael: Oh okay. Well I was wondering if you felt safe to leave? Is your tank filled? Do you tires have air? Are any of your engine lights on?

I tilt my head at the phone, resisting the urge to smile.

Noelle: Uh, I'm seventy percent sure that all of these are taken care of.

Michael: Please check before you leave, and if anything is wrong give me a call so that I can come help you out.

Noelle: Thanks Michael, I will.

Michael: Don't forget.

All my depressing thoughts were gone as I stood with an extra pep in my step. I gathered my things, not even bothering to shower and head out of the building.

I checked the time, and it was two in the morning.

The parking lot was empty, and quiet, and maybe I shouldn't have walked out here alone.

As I unlock my car, I check my tires, my gas, and stared at my dashboard for a long time trying to figure out if anything was wrong.

Since Michael had it repaired not too long ago, everything was still up to par.

Noelle: I'm all good. I'll let you know when I'm home.

The drive home was filled with pleasant thought, and now and then I found myself laughing at things Michael said, or smiling at the way he made me feel.

Even after our very first date, I felt like I was walking on air – and I know this is supposed to be expected as we're in our honey moon phase and all but . . . I haven't felt this way in a long time.

10- "The woman was too stunned to speak"

"What is this?"

I hold up a box, and my aunt Cleo snatches it out of my hands.

As I stand on the porch, I place both hands on my hips and narrow my eyes at her.

"Don't tell me it's another gift from your, boss."

I follow her inside, shutting the door behind me as she sighs loudly.

"Stay out of grown folks business, miss Noelle," she yells, trying to escape into her room.

"Fine, then I guess all of my juicy details from my date yesterday will remain within me."

Aunt Cleo pauses, turning around with a defeated face.

"Fine, we'll open it, together."

I clap happily, plopping onto the couch and tapping the seta next to me.

She silently cusses me out under her breath but of course I ignore her.

As she opens up the box, I try to get an early look by sitting up straight.

"You keep doing that," she snorts, "you gonna end up looking like a duck."

"Hilarious," I tell her dryly, "just hurry up."

"I'm wondering if they sent this package to me or you."

She finally pulls out the box, and inside of it with a necklace and ring set. My mouth drop open at the size of the diamonds.

"Uh . . . Auntie, are you 100% sure that you and this man don't got anything going on on the sidelines?"

"I –" usually she'd be quickly to defend herself but even she had to take a breath after seeing the diamonds.

She quickly shut the cases, while rubbing her head.

I watch, confused as she placed the items back in the box, "what're you doing?"

"This, is too much, Noelle," she spoke to me, but it seemed like she was trying to convince herself, "I mean I can accept th-the designer bags, shoes, even the robes, I can deal with dresses, and even expensive chocolate but there's no way that this man spent over a hundred thousand on me."

"How do you know the price?"

"We recently invested in this jewelry business, this was one of the most expensive pieces, and admittedly, I may have mentioned that it's a beautiful set. But I didn't want him to buy it for me!"

"Okay, let's calm down then," I tell her, "why is this a bad thing?"

"Because,' she stares at me incredulously, as if I was already supposed to know, "he's my boss, Noelle. He can't – I can't- accept -,"

"But you've already accepted so many other things," I raise an eyebrow, genuinely confused, "besides the price tag, I guess, what make this so different."

The issue here was obviously not the price of the items, not even the item itself, as I started at Aunt Cleo, I realized that she was . . . afraid.

I didn't know what to say to her then, but she stood and continued to close up the box.

"This is just too much," she mutters before she leaves for her room, and shuts the door behind her.

I felt terrible.

She always knew what to say when I got in my head and there she was being consumed by her mind and I didn't even say anything.

With a sigh, it ae the box and open it up again only this time I noticed a piece of paper at the bottom.

I don't know if you are tired as I am,

But I'm tired of waking up every day, missing you, but not being able to tell you,

I'm tired of listening to your laugh, watching your smile, and not being able to genuinely tell you that . . . I'm in love with you.

My eyes widen at this man's confession, and I rest a palm on my lips, reading on,

I will be in the city tomorrow, and it is my hopes that I am able to meet you,

and tell you all these these things in person.

Clementine, if you didn't' see it the first time, I am utterly in love with you

And I cannot stand another moment, not being able to tell you

I await your call . . .

Evanio.

#

With everything going on, I almost forgot about my date.

In fact, I forgot about Michael completely.

I hadn't texted him last night, and when I woke up it was because the doorbell rang for the package and well . . . you know how that went.

Evanio was coming to the city, for my Aunt Clementine and she didn't even know. I considered telling her, but I didn't know how she would react and the last thing I wanted was for her to feel worse.

I did her a favor by taping the note onto the box, and retreating into the safety of my room, where I was now trying to contact Michael.

When my texts went unanswered, I tried calling but it went straight to voicemail.

It was a little after three, and having not heard from him today, I wasn't sure if I should've got ready or not.

Finally, just as it was about to hit 4 o'clock, he called back. I had never picked up the phone faster in my life.

"Hey," I rasp and I hear shuffling on the other end.

"Hey," he replies, and it goes quiet.

"Uh – I'm sorry I didn't call . . . or text last night I was exhausted."

"Despite the fact you had me up worried and that's why I'm waking up at four in the afternoon, you're forgiven."

"Oh no," I coo, placing a hand on my forehead and shutting my eyes, "what time did you go to sleep?"

"I ended up falling a sleep at 5 in the morning," he confesses with a sigh, and more shuffling is heard, "I thought about calling you but I didn't want to push."

"I'm sorry," I breathe, "I didn't know you would've . . ."

"It's okay, it's just after the incident, it makes me feel better when I know you're home safe."

A feel utter warmth cover my heart as his words, and my stomach swims with butterflies.

"I get that, from now on, I won't forget, and if I do . . . don't be afraid to call."

"Roger that," he replies, breaking into a yawn and I hear the tap turn on.

"So . . . should we rain check for out date?"

"Yeah, absolutely not. I'm running a bit late but I'll be there."

I bite my lip to continue my grin, hugging my pillow to my chest.

"Great, let me go get ready then."

"I'll see you soon, later?"

"Later . . ."

He hangs up, and I end up locking eyes with myself in the mirror.

I was a giddy mess.

Michael did not have to be this amazing. If I wasn't careful I would fall hard onto my ass.

As I let out a breath, I try to forget about everything so that I could get ready for date number 2.

#

"Did you check the schedule?"

When Michael pulled up I ran outside to meet him there because I knew he'd walk up to the door and I didn't really want to disturb my aunt from whatever she was doing in her room.

We were currently on our way to the movies, and I must admit, casual wear looked really good on him.

"I didn't, but I'll have it done now."

He nods in response.

"'The Addams Family 2' is playing in about 10 minutes."

"What it is?"

"I have no idea," I chuckle, "but it' animated . . . so . . ."

"Alright then, we can watch it."

I purchase the tickets for us online, and sit back to enjoy the rest of the ride.

"I take it you didn't get any work done today?'

"I didn't," he sighs, "but that's okay, besides new scents there's nothing much to do."

"Did you sleep well last night? How was work?"

"Uh . . . it was really crowded. We danced for a full hour straight because of how many people there were, my feet felt like they were on fire."

"I guess that excuses you not texting me," he narrows his eyes at my playfully from the side and I grin.

"Again, I am super sorry about that."

"Nah, don't sweat it," he shakes his head, "I'm just glad that you're here."

Once again, my heart is coated with a thick, warm blanket as I stare at this man. What was he trying to do to me?

I don't have time to respond because we arrive at the cinema.

He parks swiftly before stepping out and pulling my door open. I take his outstretched hand, and he shuts the door behind me as we head into the building.

Once in I show them the ticket IDs on my phone.

"You paid for them already?"

"I did, yeah," as I slip my phone back into my purse, I noticed that Michael's face had changed.

"Why? Is something wrong?"

"When I'm with you, you don't have to pay for anything."

"Oh – I just – well I just bought them automatically because I was already on the website –"

"Okay," he shrugs, "then next time ask for my card."

Michael continues to lead me towards the snack section, and I tried my best not to let my mouth drop open.

My first attempt at choosing a man, and I get all of this.

Please universe, don't embarrass me and make this too good to be true.

We purchase our snacks and get seated in the theatre.

I had a hot dog and some nachos with extra cheese, as well as a large coke. I absoluetely loved the movie's cups, there were so big!

Michael just took some popcorn, and a water and honestly I expected nothing more.

The movies starts up, the theatre is practically filled.

This is the part I hate the most. Later comers tiptoeing in, and you having to twist and turn in your chair to accommodate them. And don't get me started on those family's of ten.

Maybe we shouldn't have chosen a family movie.

"Are you okay?" Michael whispers, and I nod in response. He takes my hand from my lap, and engulfs it with his before leaning back in his chair, and staring at the big screen.

Meanwhile, I was busy staring at him.

\#

A/N:

Hey guys, how are you doing?

As most of you know, I'm signed to Dreame, so the rest of this novel will be on there.

If you have no problem with that, here's the link:

https://www.starywriting.com/novel/RwYoWMj2Uu2u7sVS8BNZzg%3D%3D.html

it'll be FREE for a long while.

And if you do, then thank you so much for supporting me, and reading this far. I really hope than in the future I'm able to write freely on Wattpad again. XoXo, Zoe